Rata-pata-scata-fata

A Caribbean Story

by Phillis Gershator   Pictures by Holly Meade

STAR BRIGHT BOOKS

NEW YORK

Author's Note

Rata-pata-scata-fata is an old-time Virgin Islands way of talking nonsense — Caribbean gobbledy-gook. It might be imitation Spanish, since the Islands are close to Puerto Rico, or perhaps it comes from one of the many West African languages that influenced local English Creole. At one time, there were sixteen African languages spoken in St. Thomas alone!

The conch horn the fisherman blows (conch is pronounced "conk") is made from a big, beautiful pink-and-white shellfish shell.

The "pot-fish" Junjun wishes for is a reef fish that is small enough to be caught in a fish pot — a cagelike trap — and big enough to fit in a cooking pot. The tamarinds he wishes for are the sour fruit of the tamarind tree, originally imported to the tropics from India. You can suck on tamarinds (though not too many or your tongue will hurt). They are also used in making preserves, beverages, and condiments.

Published in the United States of America by Star Bright Books, Inc., New York. The name Star Bright Books and the Star Bright Books logo are registered trademarks of Star Bright Books, Inc. Please visit www.starbrightbooks.com.

Hardback ISBN 1-932065-94-6
Paperback ISBN 1-932065-95-4

Printed in China 0 9 8 7 6 5 4 3 2 1

Library of Congress Cataloging-in-Publication Data

Gershator, Phillis.
   Rata-pata-scata-fata : a Caribbean story / by Phillis Gershator ; illustrated by Holly Meade.
      p. cm.
   Summary: Preferring to dream away the days on his Caribbean island, little Junjun tries saying magic words to get the chores done.
   ISBN 1-932065-94-6
   [1. Caribbean Area--Fiction.] I. Meade, Holly, ill. II. Title.
PZ7.G316Rat 2004
[E]--dc22
                              2004008165

To Megan Tingley for the fresh start
and to David Gershator for the happy ending.
—P.G.

To my young nephew Jacob Meade,
maker of remarkable pictures,
this book is for you!
—H.M.

Junjun liked to daydream. He liked to night dream.
And he liked to dream in between, when the birds sang
and the lizards came out to bask in the morning sun.

But Junjun's dreams were often interrupted.
There was always so much work to do!

One morning, early, his mother called, "Junjun, wake up! Don't you hear the fisherman blowing his conch horn? Quick, run across town to the market and buy us a fresh pot-fish for dinner."

"Oh, Mommy, I was busy listening to the birds," said Junjun, yawning. "I wish the fish would run across town to our house instead."

"Fish don't have legs, child."

"What if I close my eyes and say a magic word, like
rata-pata-scata-fata, three times?"

"Silly Junjun! Come now."

Junjun's mother couldn't stand around and listen to nonsense talk.
She had clothes to wash.

Junjun sat in the yard and squeezed his eyes shut.
He wished hard for a fish to swim across town.
He whispered, "Rata-pata-scata-fata" slowly, once, then again:

"Rata-pata-scata-fata,

rata-pata-scata-fata."

Then he waited for his wish to come true.

Down at the beach, the last fisherman had hauled in his traps and pulled his boat onto shore. He was late for the morning market, so he took a shortcut past Junjun's house. Rushing along, he didn't even notice a fish wiggle-waggle right out of his basket. *Floomp!*

When Junjun opened his eyes, what did he see on the dusty road?

A fish! And what did he say?
"My wish came true!"

Junjun's mother was happy with the nice wiggly fish. "But Junjun,"
she asked, "Why is the fish dusty? Did you drop it?"

"No, Mommy. The fish got dusty when it swam across town to
our house."

"What an imagination! Time to fetch the goat now, while I clean the fish. And don't forget your hat. The sun is hot, hot, hot."

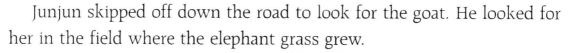

Junjun skipped off down the road to look for the goat. He looked for her in the field where the elephant grass grew.

He looked down, and he saw an alligator lizard slithering through the grass. He looked up, and he saw a chicken hawk circling overhead. He looked straight ahead, and he saw a mongoose sitting on its hind legs, still and watchful. But he didn't see the goat.

"I can't find the goat," Junjun said to the mongoose. "I wish the goat would find *me*. What if I close my eyes and say a magic word, like *rata-pata-scata-fata*, three times?"

So Junjun sat down in the grass and closed his eyes. He wished hard for the goat to come and find him.

He whispered, "Rata-pata-scata-fata," slowly, once, then again:

"Rata-pata-scata-fata,

rata-pata-scata-fata."

Then he waited for his wish to come true.

The goat had been keeping her eye on Junjun's little straw hat all along. She liked tender straw much better than tough elephant grass. As soon as Junjun sat down, the goat crept up to him, closer and closer.

Nibble, nibble, munch!

When Junjun opened his eyes, who did he see with a mouthful of straw? The goat! And what did he say?

"My wish came true!"

His mother met him on the way home. "There you are! And you found the goat."

"No, Mommy, the goat found me."

"Oh, I see. Same thing, Junjun. Good thing, too, because it's lunchtime."

When the heat of the day passed, the old tamarind tree cast its shade across the yard. Junjun liked to hop around in the late afternoon sun and watch his own shadow grow longer, like a tree.

"Don't go running after your shadow, Junjun," his mother said. "I have something to show you." She pointed up at the tree. "See those birds peck-peck-pecking at the fruit? That means the tamarinds are ripe and ready to pick."

"But Mommy, the sugar birds aren't eating tamarinds like the other birds. Maybe the fruit is too sour."

"Sour it is, Junjun, but the thrushees like it. So you'd better pick some tamarinds before the greedy thrushees eat them all."

The tree was tall. Junjun knew he'd have to climb high, high up to pick the tamarinds.

"I wish the tamarinds would pick themselves," Junjun said.

"Sure enough sure they won't," said his mother.

"What if I close my eyes and say a magic word, like
rata-pata-scata-fata, three times?"

But Junjun's mother couldn't stand around and listen to
nonsense talk. She had dinner to prepare.

Junjun closed his eyes. He wished hard for the tamarinds to pick
themselves. He whispered, "Rata-pata-scata-fata" slowly, once, then
again: "Rata-pata-scata-fata, rata-pata-scata-fata."

Just then, with a *whoosh!* a big wind blew across the island. It knocked over the empty rain barrel. It tore the sheets off the line. It shook the trees. It shook the tamarind tree so hard, the tamarinds broke loose from the branches and fell to the ground. Then the big wind blew away — phweee! — back to the sea, where it had come from.

When Junjun opened his eyes, what did he see in his basket?

Tamarinds! And what did he say?
"My wish came true!"

He carried the basket full of tamarinds into the house.

"Junjun, you picked so many!" his mother exclaimed.

"I didn't even have to climb the tree, Mommy. Sure enough sure, the tamarinds picked themselves."

"Are you making up stories again?" she said. "Now, hand me that sugar, and let's make some jam."

They peeled the thin brown shells off the tamarinds and boiled the sticky fruit in sugar water. Junjun did all the tasting to make sure the jam wasn't too sweet or too sour. Before the sun went down, they sealed up the last jar.

"Junjun," his mother said, "just one more job for
you today. It's dry, dry, dry — not a drop of rain for
days — and the rain barrel is empty. Go and fetch
some water from the well."

"I'm tired, Mommy. I wish the water would
fetch itself."

"That's a sight we'll never see," said his mother.
She sat down in the big rocking chair on the porch
and lifted Junjun onto her lap. "I'm tired, too, Junjun.
We've had a busy day. Now," she sighed, "if it would
only rain, no one would have to fetch water. Oh,
how I wish it would rain!"

"Mommy, why don't you close your eyes and say
rata-pata-scata-fata three times? Then your wish will come true."

Junjun's mother laughed, but she leaned back and
closed her eyes.

"Rata-pata-scata-fata," she sang softly.

"Rata-pata-scata-fata, rata-pata-scata-fata."

And what do you think
happened that night?

It rained!

The drops fell on the tin roof and into the empty rain barrel, lightly tapping out the rain's own song:

Ra-ta-pa-ta-sca-ta-fa-ta,

ra-ta-pa-ta-sca-ta-fa-ta,

ra-ta-pa-ta-sca-ta-fa-ta,

all night long.